Pick a Job
ANY JOB

Morgan Miller

Illustrated by
Barbara Đokić

Young Authors Publishing

Young Authors Publishing
www.youngauthorspublishing.org

Book Design by April Mostek

Our books may be purchased in bulk
for promotional, educational, or business use.
Please contact Young Authors Publishing by email at
info@youngauthorspublishing.org.

Acknowledgments

From the dreamers to the realist, for people big and small... remember the importance between living for work and simply loving what you do.

This book belongs to

_____

"Why are we here again?" questioned Aaron.

"Well, Aaron, we are because there is something I want to show you. You need to choose a career," his dad responds as they continue walking up the front steps of the building.

"Hey there, nice to see another kid here. I'm Aaron and I'm currently being dragged into some building by my dad in hopes that I'll find a 'suitable career,'" Aaron explained.

"See, I went to the career fair at school but I couldn't decide on what booth I wanted to go to. My classmates kept teasing me, saying I was better off not working at all and I should be more like my dad. I couldn't take it anymore, so I asked my teacher if I could leave and she called my dad to come pick me up. I told him what happened and he said he knew a place that could help."

"Long story short, we ended up here and
I have absolutely no idea why."

"Come along, Son. The sooner we get in, the sooner we
can leave and grab something to eat," says Aaron's dad.

"Coming Dad!" Aaron exclaimed.

"Excuse me, do you have any available guides
to take us on a quick tour?" asked his dad.

"Sure, right this way, Sir," the desk lady motioned.

Aaron paused. "Wait, you're the guide?"

Smirking, Aaron's dad replied, "I told you in
the car they work a little differently here, just
stay close and don't touch anything."

"I really appreciate you doing this Ms. ..."
he waited for her to chime in.

"KJ" she stated, "but drop the 'Ms.' I
never cared for it anyway."

"Now follow me down this hall toward our exhibits. We've got things to see and places to be!"

"Excuse me, but what exhibits are you talking about?" asked Aaron.

"Well, this is a career museum. Here, we don't focus on the policemen, teachers, or businessmen. Instead, we showcase the... less popular."

"Woah... Dad, are you seeing this?!"

"Incredible right? I thought you might like it."

"Over there is our rodeo clown, and to the right, a
professional sleeper! You'll also see our hair boiler
and cloud collector farther down," says KJ.

"And last but not least, we have our most prized exhibits. Here's our space travel agent who helps with intergalactic travel by rocket, and our scuba diving pizza delivery man who is delivering my pizza as we speak."

"This... is... AWESOME!" shouts Aaron.

"So, how does someone get a job like
this?" asks Aaron's dad to KJ.

"Are you asking for your son or yourself?"

"Ye— I mean, no! For him, definitely not asking for myself."

"Whatever you say, Sir," laughs KJ.

"Holy guacamole! These jobs are so much cooler than the ones at the fair!" shouts Aaron. "Maybe I should do one of these instead. What do you think, Dad?"

"I think it's a great idea, Aaron. So good that I might change my job too!"

"Well butter me up and call me a biscuit!"

"You really mean it Dad?"

"Yes, I really mean it! I think today is my last day
working for my boss, he drives me nuts!"

Leaving the museum, Aaron and his dad have a new understanding on life. "Thanks for showing us around, KJ! We'll try to come back soon!"

"See you around, Kid!" waves KJ.

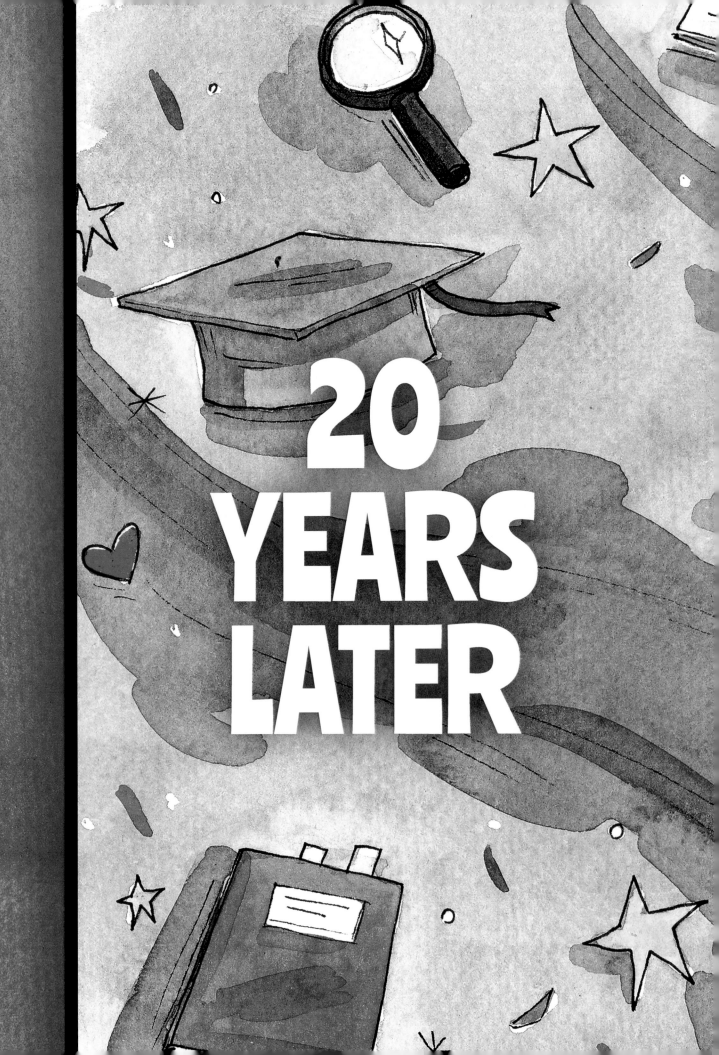

Where are they now?

No longer searching for a career, Aaron makes his own path, becoming the very rich CEO of PAX. They're known for packaging and delivering anything, anywhere, anytime.

After a few talks with KJ, his dad became the museum's most prized exhibit, the owner of a famous lemonade stand. What are the odds?

About the Author

Morgan Miller is a 13-year-old girl from Atlanta, GA. She has a loving family and an adorable puppy named Jaxon, also known as Q-Tip! She enjoys reading anything she can get her hands on and has a deep love of music.

ABOUT YOUNG AUTHORS PUBLISHING

We believe that all kids are story-worthy!

Young Authors Publishing is a children's book publisher that exists to share the diverse stories of Black and Brown children.

How We're Different

Young Authors participate in a 1-month 'Experience Program' where they are paired with a trained writing mentor that helps them conceptualize and write their very own children's book. Once their manuscript is completed, our young authors attend workshops to learn the fundamentals of financial literacy, entrepreneurship, and public speaking in an effort to ensure they have the tools they need to succeed as successful published writers. Young Authors Publishing is on a mission to empower the authors of tomorrow, using their words to change the dialogue around representation in literature.

Learn more about our impact at
www.youngauthorspublishing.org